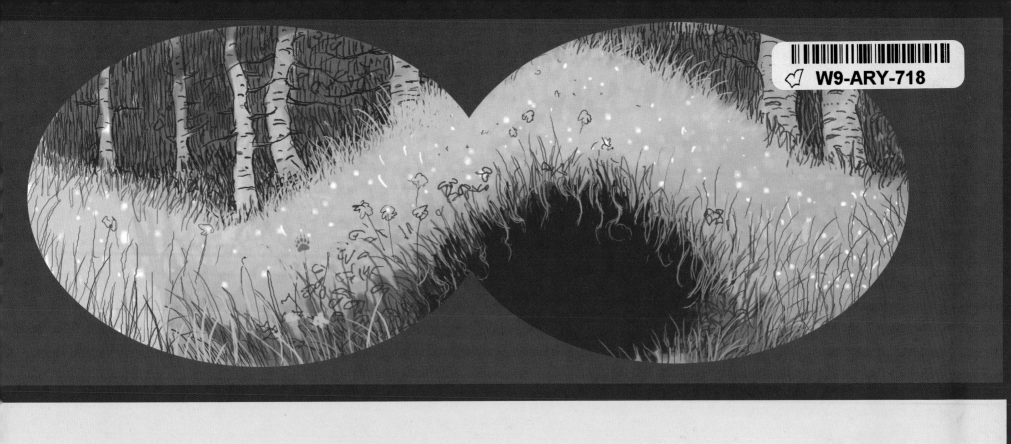

To the Sherwood Foundation and my Nebraska friends: Nancy Larimer,
Beverly Kay Doeschot, Laura Pietsch, Kathleen Day, Stephany Albritton,
Stacy Sanders, Sherry Bergen, and Kim McCain

Published by Charlesbridge
85 Main Street
Watertown, MA 02472
(617) 926-0329
www.charlesbridge.com

Library of Congress Cataloging-in-Publication Data
Biedrzycki, David, author.
   Breaking news: bear alert/reported by David Biedrzycki.
   pages cm
   Summary: In this story (told in the form of a
   television broadcast), bears emerge from
   hibernation demanding to be fed.
   ISBN 978-1-58089-663-4 (reinforced for library use)
   ISBN 978-1-58089-664-1 (softcover)
   ISBN 978-1-60734-742-2 (ebook)
   ISBN 978-1-60734-628-9 (ebook pdf)
   1. Bears—Juvenile fiction. 2. Television broadcasting—
   Juvenile fiction. [1. Bears—Fiction. 2. Television
   broadcasting—Fiction. 3. Humorous stories.]
   I. Title. II. Title: Bear alert.

   PZ7.B4745Br 2014
   813.54—dc23   2013022796

   Printed in China
   (hc) 10 9 8 7 6 5 4
   (sc) 10 9 8 7 6 5 4 3 2 1

   Illustrations done in Adobe Photoshop
   Display type set in The Sans by Luc as de Groot
   Text type set in Stripwriter by Typotheticals
   Color separations by KHL Chroma Graphics, Singapore
   Printed by Imago in China
   Production supervision by Brian G. Walker
   Designed by Diane M. Earley

WE INTERRUPT THIS
STORY TO BRING YOU

BREAKING NEWS

BEAR ALERT

Reported by **David Biedrzycki**

BEAR ALERT SKYCAM 3 NEWS HELICOPTER SHOWS TWO

BEARS ON TOP OF TRUCK HEADED DOWNTOWN.

TRAFFIC CAMERA CAPTURES SHOWDOWN. *BEAR ALERT*

BEAR ALERT BEARS SEEN ENTERING TEDDY'S DINER.

WITNESSES SAY THEY DID NOT WAIT TO BE SEATED.

Teddy's Diner security video

Porridge
Too Hot, Too Cold, or Just Right

Sal's Blueberry Pie

Bear Tracks Ice Cream

Marmalade Sandwich

GOLDIE

BEAR ALERT BEARS REPORTEDLY DEMANDED TO BE FED.

TEDDY'S CLASSIC "HUNGRY AS A BEAR" BURGERS
THE CUB FOR THE KIDDOS
THE KOALA SERVED WITH VEGEMITE
THE BROWN BEAR WITH BACON
THE PANDA WITH BAMBOO SHOOTS
THE POLAR BEAR WITH ICE CREAM
CAT BURGLARS AT LARGE
IS YOUR HOME SAFE?
I ALMOST HAD A HEART ATTACK, I WAS SO SCARED! THOSE BEARS HAD NO MANNERS, AND THEY PAID ME WITH ACORNS.
GOLDIE
MRS. LOCKS
Waited on Bears
THEY DID NOT LEAVE A VERY GOOD TIP. BEAR ALERT

ENTER

Pooh St.

Main

WET CEMENT

CAUTION CAUTION CAUTION

DETOUR
BEAR RIGHT

BEAR ALERT SKYCAM 3 NEWS HELICOPTER SPOTS BEARS

ROUNDING THE CORNER OF POOH AND MAIN.

THESE BEARS ARE WILD AND COULD BE EXTREMELY DANGEROUS.

Main Street sidewalk camera

LOUD SOUNDS WILL SCARE THEM AWAY. *BEAR ALERT*

BEAR ALERT RESIDENTS ARE ASKED TO KEEP THEIR

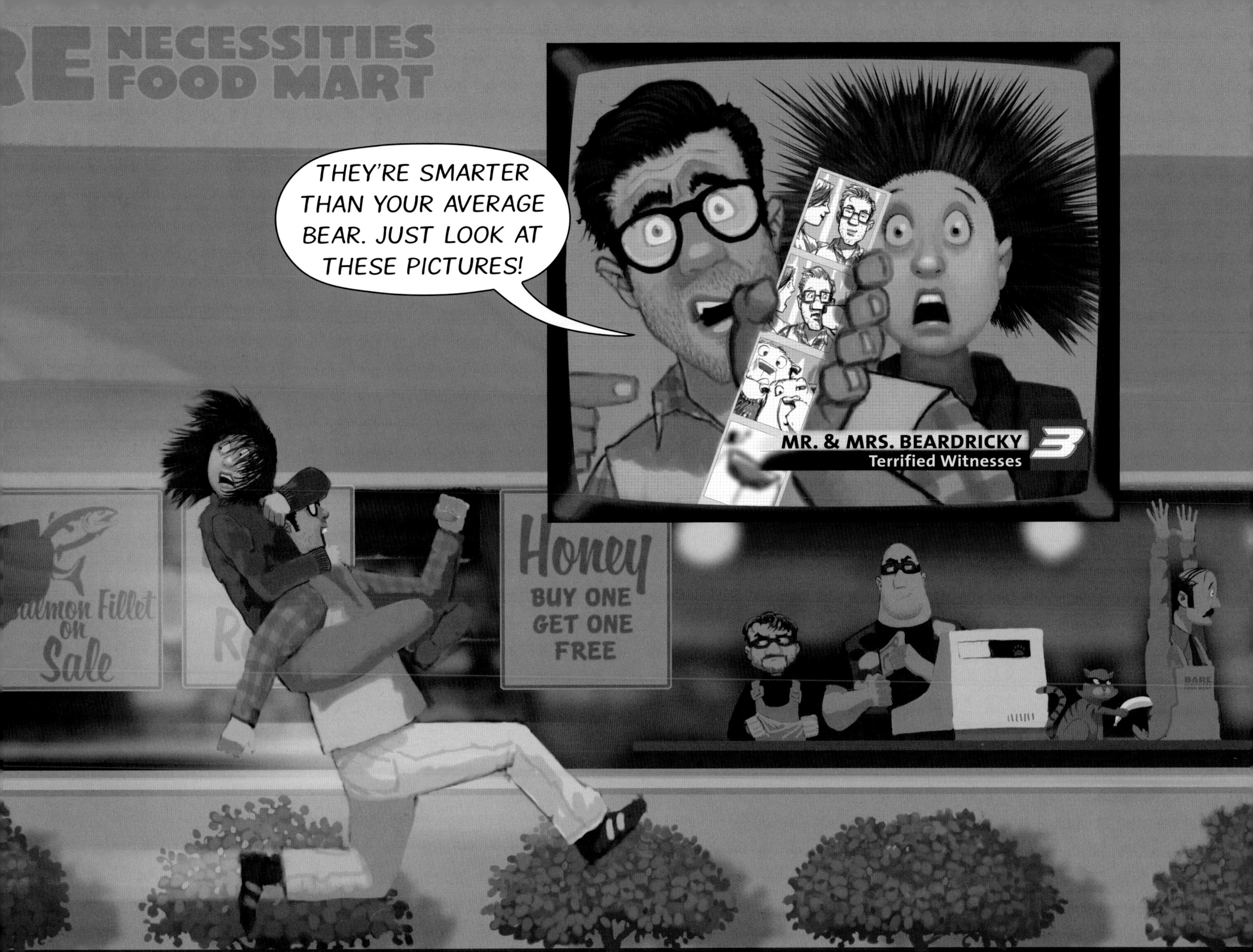

DISTANCE AND REPORT ANY UNUSUAL ACTIVITY.

BEAR ALERT ANIMAL CONTROL OFFICERS HAVE ARRIVED

Paddington's security video

BEAR ALERT BEARS LAST SEEN IN MISSES AND PETITES

SECTION OF PADDINGTON'S DEPARTMENT STORE.

BREAKING NEWS REPORTED BURGLARY AT PADDINGTON'S.

SKYCAM 3 SPOTS SUSPECTS FLEEING ON FOOT.

BREAKING NEWS BEARS NAB BURGLARS. SKYCAM 3

SHOWS POLICE CLOSING IN TO MAKE ARREST.

BREAKING NEWS CROWD APPLAUDS DEPARTING BEAR HEROES.

WE NOW RETURN YOU TO YOUR REGULARLY SCHEDULED STORY.

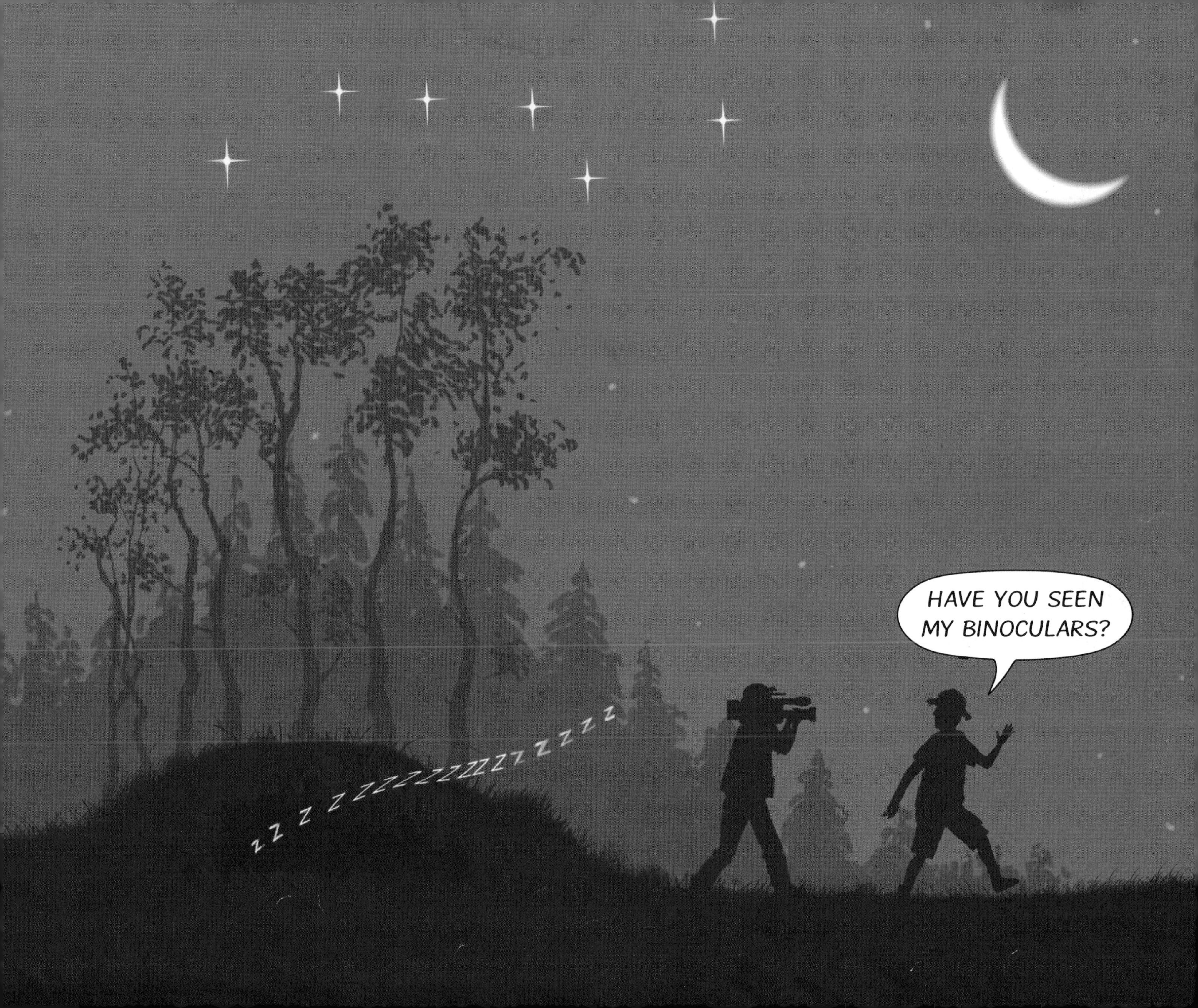
HAVE YOU SEEN MY BINOCULARS?

H.D

To Samhita..
Bear with me !! :(

[signature] 2014